for
Brodie

An inspirational story
about going inside...
discovering love,
courage and friendship

This book was inspired by the teachings of

Brandon Bays

Many of the techniques from
The Junior Journey and The Journey
are incorporated throughout this book.

I am deeply grateful to Brandon
for showing me the path to inner peace,
joy and freedom.

To find out more about the awakening,
healing work of The Journey and
The Junior Journey go to
www.thejourney.com

Written & illustrated by
Cazzie Pitsis

An Angel in my Heart

Out beyond the stars, far, far away, in the great ocean of love and light, a little soul was filled with joy and excitement because the time had come for it to make the long journey to Earth.

A shimmering spirit with a kind face and magnificent wings asked the little soul,

'Why are you going down to Earth?'

'To bring joy, love and light
to the world, of course!'

The radiant spirit helped the little soul to choose just the right family to be born into. Smiling lovingly, she gently released it to travel in a

blaze of
golden sparks
down through the
and down universe
to
the
Earth.

Nine months later, in the wee hours of the morning,
Sally and the little soul pushed and pushed together until
finally the tiny treasure entered the world and gulped its
first breath. Sally and John cried tears of joy
as they held their newborn.

It's a beautiful boy!

They had waited so long for a child.

As they gazed upon their new baby boy their hearts burst
with love and gratitude for this precious gift.
They named him Brodie.

He was already bringing

joy, love and light!

Brodie grew from a baby to a toddler, and a toddler to a boy. He felt extremely loved, and his days were filled with joyful fun and happiness.

But at night, as he lay in his bed, he was unable to sleep. It wasn't just the pains in his tummy that kept him awake, he was scared, sometimes terrified. He was sure a

big scary monster

with **huge** teeth lived under his bed.

He could hear it, some nights, creeping out.

He could feel it sitting on his bed!

His whole body would tense up as sharp pains stabbed his belly. He'd pull the covers up over his head and pray that the monster wouldn't see him.

Brodie **never** told anyone about the monster.

He was sure they wouldn't believe him. He didn't want people to think he was a scaredy-cat, or to tease him. So he kept quiet, feeling scared and alone in his bed.

Today something wonderful was about to happen, something magical. It was Brodie's 6th birthday.

There was such excitement in the air. Sally had baked a 'spantabulous' birthday cake—covered in chocolate icing and sprinkled with white fairy dust. And on the top were 6 brightly coloured glistening candles.

Brodie took a huge breath in, ready to blow them out and make his wish. He already knew what he would wish for...

...a new friend

His best friend had moved away, and Brodie missed him. So, as he blew out the candles
with all his might, he wished

'Please send me a new friend!'

Sally felt Brodie's wistfulness so she suggested a walk in the rainforest together, to brighten him up.

On the way she told Brodie about the many different kinds of insects, birds and animals that live in the forest. Then, in a hushed voice, she whispered

'There's also strange mischievous creatures like pixies, fairies and watersprites that make their home in the rainforest. Some are so magical and mysterious they haven't even got a name. If we're very patient, quiet and still we might be lucky enough to see them.

They're so small. They live under the rocks and leaves, and in the trees and bushes. Some even live in the water. They are so secretive…

only those who really believe
in them can see them!'

As three beautiful bright butterflies danced by, Brodie wondered if fairies and pixies flew like butterflies?

He stopped to look for mysterious creatures in the fallen leaves, under moss-covered rocks, and behind the roots of the ancient trees. Slowly he fell further behind.

What was that strange noise coming from the undergrowth?

oueeeeeeeeeeeeeeeeeeeeeeee

Brodie glimpsed something out of the corner of his eye.

'Maybe it's a pixie' he thought, as he left the path. Creeping quietly, following the sound, he was moving further and further away from the track. He stopped, looked around, but he didn't know where he was

He was lost!

A sharp stabbing pain was growing in his tummy as he realized he was all alone.

'What if the monster followed me here and he finds me? I'll die in the forest and no one will know where I am. I'll never see my mum and dad again.'

He curled up into a ball inside a big tree root and began to cry.

Trembling amid the tree roots he wished he hadn't gone off alone.

The pain in his tummy was almost unbearable.

Would mum and dad find him soon?

With his eyes tightly shut he sobbed.

He was cold and hungry too.

He cried until there were no tears left...

In the empty stillness, he felt a soft touch upon his shoulder.

'Mum!' he cried, happy she had found him at last.

But when he opened his eyes he could hardly believe what he saw. Standing before him was the most beautiful angel he had ever seen. She was filled with a soft golden light.

He felt surrounded by love and very safe in her presence.

He wondered

'Who is she? Where did she come from?
Why is she here?'

And without her even speaking, he heard her whisper

'You wished for a new friend
and here I am.
I'm actually a very old friend
even though you don't remember me.'

Amazed, Brodie asked his new friend where she lived.
She softly replied

'My name is Damara,
and I live in your heart.

When you want to talk to me, close your
eyes and breathe into the love in your heart.
There you'll find me sitting by a fire.
Come and sit with me!
You'll always feel safe and loved by the fire.

I've always been in your heart.
We were friends before you were born.
I came down to earth with you and
I've been by your side ever since.

I sit by your bed at night hoping you'll
remember me. What you thought was a
monster was only me kissing you goodnight.
No one but you can see me.'

Brodie was so glad Damara was with him.
He felt comforted to know

he was no longer alone.

Damara softly and lovingly held Brodie in her arms.
He felt a soothing warmth spread throughout his body.
The ache in his tummy disappeared as he began to relax.
Brodie knew he still needed to find his way back, but
he didn't know which way to go.
Damara was there, especially to help him, with her

magical bright balloons

She explained that each balloon was filled with wonderful
qualities such as relaxation, peace and fun.
If he breathed them in they'd become part of him.

'The red balloon is full of courage.

The orange balloon will help you know it's safe
to speak out and express how you really feel

The blue balloon is full of self-trust.

The pink balloon is filled with your mum's
and dad's love.

The purple balloon will place an invisible
crystal dome around you to keep you safe
from harm.

I'm sure these will help you' smiled Damara.

Closing his eyes, Brodie breathed in a huge breath from each balloon, one at a time.

He tingled all over as he let the qualities of each balloon fill his whole body. Breathing in the last balloon he noticed that he didn't feel scared anymore.

He felt courageous
He felt loved
He knew he was safe

He trusted himself to find his way back to the path, and back to his mum and dad.

He was sure his mum and dad were looking for him too.

His body felt
relaxed and strong

The hollowness in his tummy was gone because he didn't need to be scared anymore.

Hand in hand with Damara, Brodie seemed to naturally know which way to go.

And before he knew it, they stumbled back upon the path.

Standing on the track Brodie knew he could now find his OWN way back to his mum and dad.

He felt like a real explorer—strong, grown up and adventurous.

Damara asked Brodie to promise to tell his mum and dad how he had felt when he was lost.

'It's really important we share our feelings.
It's safe to let people know
how we feel, even when we are afraid.'

Smiling, she told Brodie to remember she was always waiting for him in his heart, by the fire.

She gave him a soft kiss and

melted

back

into his
heart

Brodie looked up the path.

He could hear his mum calling his name

The sound of her voice was easy to follow.

As if flying on angel's wings he raced around the bend, and with his heart pounding, he ran into her open arms.

> 'I was so scared. I thought you would stop looking for me and I would be all alone in the forest and I might never find you.'

Sally and John told Brodie they would search to the ends of the earth until they found him.

> 'I was more scared than when I thought the monster was hiding under my bed. But now I know there's no monster, it's my friend Damara who lives in my heart!'

Sally cried a tear of gratitude to Damara, as she held Brodie tightly to her heart.

That night, as Brodie lay in his soft warm bed, he felt safe and relaxed. The emptiness he used to feel in his tummy at night had gone.

Today he had learnt many things about himself.

He remembered he was here to bring

joy, love and light

to the world.

He quietly closed his eyes and imagined himself glowing full of light, shining his love and happiness out into his room, and then out into the world.

The monster had always been his friend.

He whispered *Damara*'s name.

In the peaceful stillness of his bed, he began to drift off to sleep. He felt a soft gentle angel kiss on his cheek.

This had been the best birthday ever!

Surrounded by love and light he floated into his heart. There, sitting by a blazing fire, was Damara waiting for him. As he settled down beside her a sleepy mist of love surrounded him.

Are you wondering who lives in your heart?
Let's see if we can find out.

So, make yourself really comfy, and close your eyes…
Take a big deep breath in… and let it out. Good… and one
more slow breath in… and let it softly out… Now, imagine
receiving four bright balloons full of wonderful qualities.
From the first balloon, breathe in the feeling of relaxation
and peace… Let in fill your whole body… And next
breathe in a balloon of trust… then a balloon of courage,
breathe that in… and then a balloon full of fun… Great.

Now imagine some stairs going downwards… there's ten
shimmering steps. It's OK if you can't see it. Just pretend.
These steps are magical because they will lead you to a very
special door. And behind this door is a bright light, filled
with love. This is the light of your own heart.

So go ahead, and step onto the top step, number 10. I wonder
what colour each of the steps are? Step onto step 9, now 8 …
and with each step feeling a tingling throughout your
body. Now step 7, hearing the sounds of your breathing,…
and now step 6, feeling relaxed. Then 5. Feeling the
shimmering steps beneath you, step onto step 4, and now 3.

Stepping onto step number 2, and when you're ready, step 1 … There in front of you is a magnificent door. It's encrusted with sparkling jewels, gold and silver. Behind this door is a blazing light, a huge presence of love (your heart) and your special friend is waiting for you.

So go ahead and open the door. Feel the warmth of the luminous light of love. Look around. Call out to your friend. Say 'I'm here!' Can you see them, or feel them? Sometimes you just know they're there. Who is it? And what are they like? It might be a super hero, or a mystical creature or a wise wizard. It can be anyone, but it will always be someone you trust and feel safe with.

Can you see them there by the fire? Go over and give your friend a hug, sit by the fire with them, and ask them to be with you tonight in your dreams. Remember, you can meet your special friend any time you like.

When you're ready say 'I'll see you again soon' and step back through the door, and back up the steps.

And if you ever feel scared at night or think you're being watched, put yourself in a crystal dome, and ask whoever you think is there to come out. It might be your special friend who is there with you, just like Brodies's friend.

Who might your special friend be?

Published in Australia by
Carol Pitsis
30 Ocean View Road Mullaway NSW 2456

National Library of Australia
Cataloguing-in-publication data

Pitsis, Cazzie.
An Angel in my Heart/written and illustrated
by Cazzie Pitsis; editor, Mouli MacKenzie.
Mullaway, NSW: C. Pitsis, 2008
ISBN 9780980379112 (pbk.)
A823.4.

Edited and designed by
Mouli MacKenzie
m@msquareddesign.com.au

Colour reproductions by Rob Little Digital Images
Printed by Goanna Print Canberra
Available from
www.angelinmyheart.com.au